A Play

Rally Car Race

Story by Annette Smith

People in the Play

Reader

Zac

Dad

Man from Next Door

Reader

Zac loved watching rally cars on TV.
One day, a man came to live next door.
He had a rally car in his garage.

Zac *(to Dad)*

The man next door owns a real rally car.
It is bright red and yellow
and it has special tyres.

Dad

Stay by the fence.
You can see the car from there.

Reader

Every weekend,
the man would bring the rally car
out of the garage.
Zac would watch him.

Reader
The man would walk around his car
and clean it.
He would look underneath it
and check the engine.
One Saturday …

Zac *(calling out)*
Please can I come and look at your car?

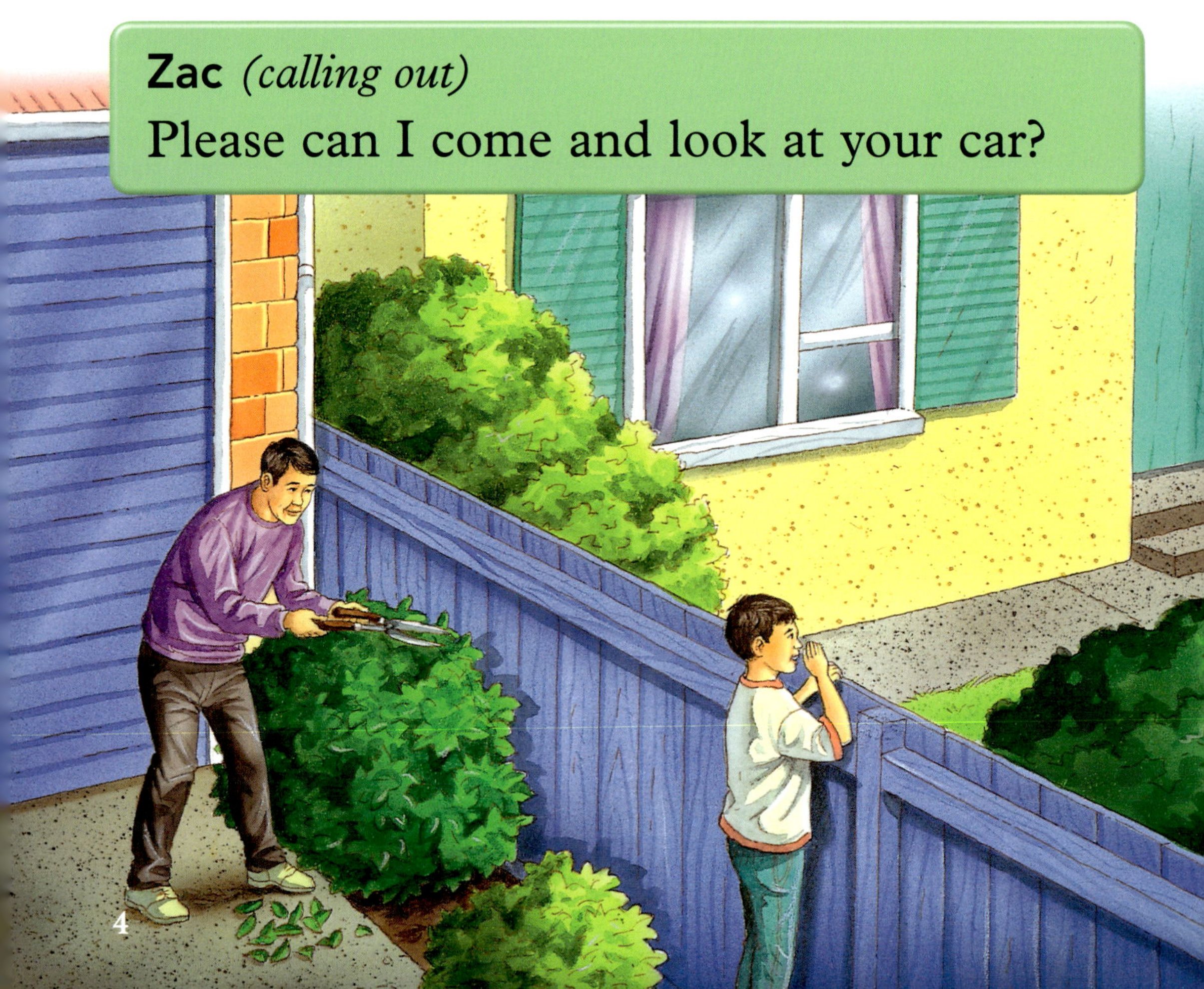

Man from Next Door *(crossly)*
No, I'm too busy.
This car is going to be in an important race next weekend.

Dad
Don't worry, Zac.
I know where that race will be held.
I'll take you to see it.

Reader

The next Saturday, Zac and his dad stood with the other people at the sideline.

Dad

Look, Zac!
The teams are getting the rally cars ready for the races.

Zac *(shouting)*
There's the man from next door!
Hello! Hello!

Reader
The man nodded at Zac
and turned away quickly.

Reader
The cars in the first race
sped off up the winding road.
Then, to Zac's surprise,
the man from next door
came running over to them.

Man from Next Door *(gasping as he speaks)*
I've forgotten my special helmet.
It's in the garage at home.
I can't race my car without it.
Could you go back and get it for me
in time for the third race, please?

Dad
Yes. We'll get the helmet for you.

Man from Next Door
Thanks! Here are the keys to the garage.

Reader

Soon, Zac and his dad were back with the man's special helmet.

Man from Next Door *(smiling)*

Thanks. My race is about to start. I hope you will come back and see me when all the races are finished.

3
1
1

Reader
Zac and his dad watched the man drive his car up the winding road.

Zac
He's going very fast.

Reader
They waited for a long time.
Then they saw a cloud of dust in the distance.

Zac *(shouting)*
Wow! Look, Dad!
The man from next door is in the lead.

NTROL

Reader

After the races had finished, the man from next door came over to Zac and Dad.

Man from Next Door

My name's Mark.
Come and see my car.
Thanks to you, I won my race.

Reader

Mark handed Zac a helmet.

Man from Next Door *(winking at Zac)*

Here. Try this helmet on, Zac.
I need a new co-driver.
Let's go for a little ride.

CONT

Reader
Zac clipped on his seatbelt
and they went around part of the track.

Zac
That was great!

Man from Next Door *(laughing)*
Yes, and please come over and help me
with my car next weekend.